Strings of the Fates

Reign of Goddesses #1.5

C.D. Britt

www.authorcdbritt.com

Cover Artwork by GermanCreative

Editing by EFC Services, LLC.

Published by C.D. Britt

ISBN (eBook): 979-8-9872432-4-4

ISBN (paperback): 979-8-9872432-5-1

Contents

To all my readers. Thank you.

CHAPTER 1

Somewhere around 3000 BCE, the Underworld

Today was the day Persephone was to become the guardian of the dead.

Standing in the hall before large wooden doors, skulls carved into the wood, she felt so small compared to the substantial palace around her. It hadn't managed to sink in yet that she was no longer a small, vulnerable human.

No, she had died and now held an incredible amount of power inside her soul.

Persephone jumped when the doors began to open but worked to put steel into her spine before anyone walked in. She worked to gather herself before all the eyes in the throne room were upon her.

Taking a deep breath, Persephone walked past the doors held open by two men who were nothing more than shadows, yet somehow substantial enough to affect the world around them. Reevkas were what she had been told they were called. Servants of the castle that took on a mortal form when in service.

No one but the reevkas who had opened the doors stood in the room.

Her bare feet stopped as she cleared the threshold, her eyes locked on the dais that held the obsidian throne humming with power. The throne that was now hers.

Once she was seated upon it, she would be one with the Underworld. A vessel of its power. A lifeline to the souls in the realm and the ones in the mortal realm yet to come.

Bonding with the Underworld was important, not just because a ruler was needed now that her father was imprisoned, but without one, everything done in his name, all the torture and chaos, would continue.

With time, the Underworld would break apart and have far-reaching consequences in all the realms.

Cronus, her father, had taken over the world and all the realms associated with it only to leave parts of it to neglect when he lost interest. However, when something held her father's interest, it was far worse.

There were many reapers in the Underworld, born into that role, but there was one she'd met when she walked her sisters past the gates that stuck with her.

He was not meant to be a reaper but was the deity of death that had been as much a victim as she and her sisters were to her father's cruel machinations. While her father had killed her and her sisters, only three of the five surviving, the reaper had been branded with runes. Runes that controlled the powerful deity, made him mindless while under Cronus's control.

A man she'd come to trust since her death, and in their mutual pain, she felt a familial bond grow between them. She wished he was here with her as she took this large and final step, cementing her future.

A step that terrified her. It meant she would be even more powerful, and after the surge of power she'd felt sending her father to Tartarus, she could understand now how such immense power could corrupt.

To have been more powerful than a man who was considered a god among gods was enough to terrify her.

She never wanted to be like her father. Never wanted it to change who she was in such a formidable fashion that she couldn't find her way back from it.

No, she was afraid of that, terrified really. Which was why standing before the throne of the Underworld and knowing the hold she would have over an entire domain caused her no small amount of fear.

At the same time, she knew how important it was that the Underworld had a guardian, but it didn't change the fact that she was terrified. Her body shook as she tried to muster the courage to take her place of power. To harness the magic of the Underworld, a place that was now hers as much as the sky was Hera's and the sea was Amphitrite's.

Roles her sisters had slipped into much easier than she was slipping into her own.

Not long ago, she'd been human, and the Underworld was all myths and folktales the people of her village spoke of, a place where their loved ones went. But she'd thought it was all for comfort, a way to acknowledge that they were more than bodies buried beneath the earth.

How could so much happen in such a short period of time? How would it feel now to know she would never die? Her memories of being human were still so fresh: helping Demeter find Hera in the forest every time she ran off and was too scared to come home in the dark, swimming with Amphitrite, and helping to keep the hearth lit with Hestia.

Now Demeter and Hestia were souls under her care as the guardian of the Underworld; their memories of their mortal lives spent together as sisters were gone after they were made to drink from the River Lethe. While Hestia and Demeter were always near, they would only see her as the goddess of the Underworld. Not as a sister. Persephone wondered what they would think of their three remaining sisters becoming something straight from the stories of their youth.

Persephone had been the one to take the Underworld for one reason alone: to walk both her sisters through the gates herself. To be the one to see them to their final resting place since she was the oldest and unable to save them.

Luckily, the two immortals currently running the realm had allowed it without question. Thanatos, the reaper and general of the Underworld's army, would have been the one to walk her sisters past the gates had Persephone not made it clear she would be doing so. Also Hecate, the deity of witchcraft and crossroads. Both of them had been working together to keep the power structure of the Underworld balanced in the absence of a guardian.

Both had stood on either side of the gates as she walked with her chin up, hands holding her sisters' hands, and tried not to shed a tear. To be strong for them as she had tried so very hard to be in life.

But in guiding her sisters past the gates, she made an unspoken promise to take the throne immediately after she had delivered her sisters. That was why she now stood before the obsidian throne made of stone that was chiseled to look like black horns on either side of the headrest. Skulls were carved into the armrests, making it look like something one would expect to find awaiting them in the Underworld.

Three steps. She needed to walk up three steps to accept her fate and take her throne.

A throne of death.

Shaking like a leaf, terrified of what would happen when she sat upon her new seat of power, she had to push herself to move closer.

Silver engulfed the room, heralding the appearance of the deity of witches and crossroads. The powerful being walked to stand beside her as her silver light dimmed and disappeared. Both of them faced the throne that would be Persephone's entire future.

Beside her, the woman with silver hair and eyes and light-brown skin smiled.

Hecate.

"I know you wanted to do this alone, but I felt like a friendly face could help." Hecate reached out and gave Persephone's hand a squeeze before letting it go. Persephone could feel a calming power moving through her from Hecate and the touch of her hand.

Closing her eyes to fight against the tears threatening to spill over, she turned away from Hecate. That Hecate had come anyway, was here in one of the most pivotal moments that would make up her entire reign, it overwhelmed her to feel as if there were more than her sisters looking out for her.

Pushing her shoulders back, Persephone remembered what she had promised herself on that first dark night after she had ascended as a goddess; never again would she cry. Her tears did nothing to stop her father from killing her and her sisters. Nothing to stop him from hunting Hera like an animal.

Tears were worthless. A waste of energy.

Taking a deep breath, Persephone stilled her shaking limbs and straightened her back with determination.

It did nothing to still the rapid beating of her heart, but not every battle could be won so easily.

Barefoot, she approached the throne, her torn dress the last memento of her mortality. The ragged hole remained from where her father had driven his knife into her, the blood on the fabric now dry and stiff, and the bottom of the dress dragging across the floor. Pushing her dull, black hair from her face, she held her breath as she stepped up onto the dais.

One step.

Two.

Three.

Turning, she looked to where Hecate stood, nodding at her to continue.

"You have no idea how much the Underworld needs you. How much we all need you." Hecate gave her a small, sad smile. Hecate also knew how the balance would change for Persephone, what she would be both gaining and losing by taking her seat upon the throne.

Bound for all eternity to both her power and the Underworld with no way to escape the responsibility without true death.

She could leave, run, and escape the Underworld to try to live a somewhat normal life among humans, but the mortal realm held nothing for her any longer. The man she was to be married to would have already moved on. No family. No friends. She would be starting over again, but immortal. Alone.

Mortality held nothing but more pain, more loss. At least this way, she would be with her sisters.

With that, she took the last steps separating her from her future. Before she could think more about it and talk herself out of it, she sat down, a little too quick, a gasp leaving her at the impact. But all too soon that gasp was for an entirely different reason.

Shadows swirled around her and through her, and though she knew inherently she should be scared, the actual feeling was soothing. Like finding a missing loved one and being held in a hug she hadn't been aware she so desperately needed.

Dispersing from her, the shadows moved to the sides of the throne room, spreading out along the floor on each side before they took the form of men.

Each one formed, one at a time, until there were two lines of them against the walls all the way back to the throne room doors. The two shadow men on either side of the doors took on their mortal forms, all of them now looked flesh and blood, as if they'd never been anything but.

Hecate stood in the middle, her hand to her mouth and tears in her eyes as she looked around the room.

The men who had just been made of shadow wore strange armor that covered their bodies. A helmet of the same metal with black skulls etched into them sat upon their heads, and they had spears at their sides with swords at their waists.

It was an army beyond any Persephone had ever seen before. She'd lived in a small village where the men were all simple farmers, so these men were out of the scope of what her imagination was capable of creating.

Smoke and shadows formed right before her, at the bottom of the dais, and then appeared the man who had guided her and her sisters away from the place they'd been struck down. The reaper who had become a brother, not in blood, but something far stronger. Who'd watched over them every day and slept outside their door every night to protect them.

Who had helped Persephone and Amphitrite find Hera so they could end their father's vile reign once and for all.

With tears in his eyes, wearing the same type of metal as the men around the room, he bowed before her and took a knee, his arm across his chest ready to make a vow. One she wasn't sure she was ready for but knew she would desperately need in her new position.

"I, Thanatos, will be your sword and shield just as I am your reaper," he announced. She watched as the brands that ran along his arms, ones that had been red and raised as if infection were settling in, began to glow. Before their eyes, each brand took on a flesh color only a fraction lighter than his olive skin.

The man she trusted, who understood as well as she did how cruel her father was, would be an ally for life.

She was mystified as the brands faded, but from the atmosphere of the room and how Hecate quietly wept, she knew it was something bigger than she could ever fathom.

Further indication of how enormous this choice was for her to make. The enormity of the choice for her to take the power the Underworld offered was.

"Stand, Thanatos," she ordered, unsure of what to say next, but something in her mind quickly filled in the words her mortal brain could never have come up with, and they flowed from her. She had a suspicion it was the Underworld, and how she knew *that* she did not know. "As your queen, I will be your light in the darkness and your anchor in all that is Chaos."

Stepping down, she was startled by the luminescent tone to her porcelain skin, her hair shining so brightly it held a blue hue. Her torn mortal dress was gone and in its place a beautiful black gown that might have been a bit more revealing than anything she'd ever worn as a human. She had the fleeting thought that she should be sad her dress was gone, the last relic of her mortal life, but something in her said she'd just gained far more than she lost.

The Underworld was now a part of her, just as she was a part of it.

Power moved through her, unimaginable in its intensity, and one thought prevailed through it all.

I will use this power to protect and never harm.

She would never become her father.

She would never become her father.

CHAPTER 2

Standing before the souls of the Underworld coming to where she was holding court, Persephone felt a pull, something in her chest tugging at her to follow. Her eyes locked with Thanatos who was speaking to some lord who had crossed over the veil to the Underworld and still thought himself of some higher importance.

The tug loosened as she rubbed at her sternum between the fabric of her black lacy dress opened down the front to her navel.

The ballroom was large, substantial, with giant black columns that lined and framed the long dance hall. A guard was stationed along each one of the columns keeping an eye on the people milling about. Blue veils were draped around the ballroom, sconces sparkling with blue fire the only lights, yet it was somehow bright enough.

Sitting on a smaller version of the throne at the front of the ballroom, Persephone felt ridiculous while people mingled and danced. Yet she knew she would feel even more uncomfortable among them. Persephone never knew what to say to these people, *her* people, so she thought it better to say nothing.

Cold. That was the word she heard the most to describe her, and while it hurt, it was far better than the alternative, them realizing the woman who held the power of the realm was nothing more than a scared and traumatized girl pretending to be what she was not.

As powerful of mind as she was of magic.

The lords and ladies, so to speak, of the Underworld mingled with each other under her watchful gaze among the trays of drinks and food brought around by the reevkas.

The tug in her chest pulled again, and it felt like something was wrapping itself around her actual heart, pulling and putting it off its rhythm. The beats were sporadic and intense as her heart worked to push through whatever was happening.

Finally catching her eyes, Thanatos raised a brow before a look of concern rolled over his face at her clutching at her chest. He was obviously not feeling the same thing, so it couldn't be a soul. Could it?

She had been in power for over five hundred years and had yet to have a soul call to her personally. Her connection to the Underworld was steady, nothing odd along that line of power, so she wasn't quite sure if a soul readying to leave its mortal coil was what was pulling at her so insistently.

Shadows were in front of her before Thanatos appeared, stepping out of them from where he had opened a portal to cross the room in what she had termed a shadow jump.

"What is wrong?" he whispered, stepping up onto the dais next to where she was sitting, still clutching at her chest as if to catch her heart should it make its way through her rib cage.

Something in the mortal world was trying to grab her attention, and whatever it was had succeeded in doing so.

"I feel a tug right here in my chest," she whispered, running her fingers lightly over where her heart thumped erratically. Looking up at Thanatos as his eyebrows furrowed, she asked him the only question she could think of. "Could it be a soul?"

Shaking his head, he tried to run a hand through his long dark hair, forgetting he had it tied back for the gala that continued on around them as if nothing significant was happening with their queen.

Persephone was feeling more and more like an inanimate object placed in the castle for them to look upon and judge. Nothing more and nothing less.

"A soul's call feels like a pull on your entire body, not just one part, but I do not know what else would have such a powerful pull than a soul awaiting a psychopomp."

"Then I shall go and see for myself," she said as she stood and began to step down off the dais, planning to shadow jump from somewhere else in the castle so as not to disturb her guests, but Thanatos grabbed her elbow to stop her.

"That is for me to attend to as your reaper."

"I am aware of what your occupation is, General," she snapped, the pressure in her chest growing beyond discomfort. Closing her eyes, she took a deep breath and opened them to find not an angry look on his face, but a sardonic one.

No one else saw his sarcastic side except her and Hecate, and since he had his back to the room, no one else could see the raised eyebrow and challenge in those frosty blue eyes.

Over time, they had become close friends, but in court, he was the general and held to a different standard than the rest. It didn't mean he wouldn't try to sneak some comment in or look to catch her off guard, though.

Hecate was floating through the room, a vision in purple as she locked eyes with Persephone, handing her glass off to a reevka before making her way to where Persephone stood with Thanatos.

"Problem?" she whispered, smiling as though to assure everyone that the secret whispers between the three most powerful people in the realm were of no concern.

"I believe a soul is calling to me instead of Thanatos." The hum in her chest intensified at her words, insistent and urgent. Persephone would not be able to keep herself back for much longer.

Cocking her head to the side, Hecate looked pensive as she took in Persephone.

"Never has that happened to someone not of reaper blood," she said, answering the question Persephone hadn't spoken aloud.

"You make it sound like it's genetic and not something a guy is branded with and forced into," Thanatos growled, and Hecate laid a hand on his upper arm, calming him. It had been five hundred years, but Thanatos was still having nightmares of his time as a puppet of Cronus.

While Thanatos was getting better each day, being reminded of Cronus and his past set something off in him that Persephone hated to see. Something she could relate to more than she wished she did.

While Thanatos was a deity of death, he wasn't always a psychopomp. There were other reapers in the realm, mindless in their acquisition of souls, almost as if mere puppets of the Underworld. They took the soul and deposited it with Charon to move down the River Styx. Or should funeral rites not have been given or a blessing, the souls were deposited on the bank. There they would wander for a minimum of a hundred years.

Before Thanatos could use the powers he had been born with in any other way, he was enslaved and used as a tool to take out Cronus's enemies.

Cronus had created the most lethal weapon: a being that could kill gods and send them to a final death.

An occupation that haunted Thanatos and most likely always would.

That he offered to be a reaper for her, to walk people the whole way through the process of death, meant a lot. Some days she wondered if it was to absolve himself somehow; other days she found comfort that should someone lose a loved one like she had, Thanatos would be there to care for them.

She didn't know the whole of his past, but until he came to her with it, she wouldn't tread where she wasn't wanted.

The pull in her chest grew to be so intense by the time she had finished her thought, her teeth were starting to chatter, making her grind down on them to keep them from making noise.

"I have to go." Persephone wasn't sure if they heard her, the shadows already pulling at her faster than her own thoughts could comprehend as she searched for where the summons had originated. Instead, she released her tight hold on her power and let it show her where to go. To show her what exactly had the power to summon the ruler of the Underworld to the mortal realm.

As her shadows dissipated, Persephone found herself standing on a muddy road in a small farming village. A village quite similar to the place she'd called home as a mortal and would run around with her sisters back in her human lifetime.

Only this one held no laughter. Empty as no mothers went about their chores and no children played at their knees.

No one was trading some root vegetable and arguing over the cost. Horses were nowhere to be seen, yet she could see fresh hoofprints in the mud.

Several of the homes had been burned, the fires out now, yet smoke still rose from the ashes telling her that it had not been long since the battle had taken place.

The lack of bodies was unnerving, but she wasn't here for anything other than the soul she could now feel nearby.

Gathering her resolve, she walked along the muddy path, knowing from the weather this was north of where her home had been in the mortal realm. Here it rained all the time in a land full of mountains and cliffs. Farming techniques were advancing enough to where the northern tribes were more able to settle and find a sustainable place to stay for the seasons.

A throbbing pulse started in her temple, her hand finding the pain and rubbing as she turned, feeling the pull strengthen in the opposite direction than she had been facing. Somewhere in one of the few remaining thatched-roof houses still standing was someone ready to pass.

Rodents squeaked out an alarm as she moved through the muddied path closer to the house.

Animals always felt death nearby, and she wondered how Thanatos could stand it. It grated at her to be shunned outside of the Underworld, a reason why she hardly bothered to ever leave. She guessed he wasn't around long enough for it to be an issue, or it truly did not bother him.

Looking down, she saw a trail of blood and focused on the soul working to free itself from its mortal shell in the home where the object of her focus had most likely been residing.

As she neared the home, two bodies lay outside. It was obvious it was the enemy, one with their throat slit, and the other had died with a sucking chest wound. Close combat meaning whoever was in the home was a trained warrior since there was not more than one strike to each of the bodies. They were dispatched quickly and efficiently.

Walking past the bodies into the one-room home, her eyes quickly found the man who had called to her. He was seated and leaning against the wall next to the hearth, struggling for breath. His clothes were made of fur, bear if she had to guess.

Eyes closed, sweat and dirt marring his brow, he tried to take a steady breath, but his bearded jaw clenched in pain.

"Who are you?" he ground out, his words flowing and translating as the Underworld's magic provided her an understanding of his foreign tongue. The Underworld always compensated for such situations, according to Thanatos, so they could communicate with the souls in their care.

"I am here to take you home."

His eyes opened, hazel with long lashes.

"I am home," he growled in response.

As she moved closer, she saw there was an arrow in his chest, but he had broken off the shaft, the fletching missing, leaving the rest of the arrow in place so he didn't bleed out.

The man knew how to avoid instant death, and she wondered if he'd seen much of that in his life.

As she kneeled beside him, he watched her warily, his hand holding his side underneath the wound.

"I am dying, then."

She nodded, wishing she could reassure him, but what was the point? Persephone wouldn't lie, it was one of her biggest pet peeves.

And why did she care? Souls came through the gates every day; this one was no different.

Yet it felt *very* different somehow. *He* was very different.

Closing his eyes, he nodded.

"So be it, then. At least I died saving my family." With his words, he clenched his jaw, his teeth grinding through the wave of pain from jostling his wound while he spoke. "Let's get on with it, then."

Sorrow filled her as she took in the room. Small beds lined up along the floor next to a larger one. Children's small toys made of stone and wood scattered about, and a blanket lay over a wooden chair near the hearth ready for story time.

A father who wouldn't be here when they returned home.

How did Thanatos handle the unfairness of the world?

"I don't want them to come back before you do this, so please." Now his eyes were pleading, a tear falling down his cheek. Her eyes moved to his as his soul started to separate, and she watched possible futures move through them. He was meant to be reborn. "I don't have the strength to not plead for my life should I see my family again before I die."

Swallowing her feelings down, she placed a hand over his chest, reaching for the ball of light that each person had inside of them. Blue lit the small home as she pulled his soul from his body, and before her stood the man in his prime, the sapphire light of his soul illuminating the room around them.

Remaining silent, unsure of what to say, she watched as he looked down at his body.

"Perhaps in death I will meet the men who thought to harm us and can kill them all over again."

For some reason, that made Persephone smile.

CHAPTER 3

Persephone decided to walk the warrior to the gates herself. He'd called out to her for a reason, so perhaps she could find out why when he went before the judges. As she bypassed Charon, the boatman only cocked his head to the side and shrugged before heading back down river.

Cerberus in his three-headed form was guarding the gates as they walked up. Fire in his eyes, he looked over the warrior soul before looking at her.

From the corner of her eye, she saw the man step back, his body going into a stance that reminded her of someone ready to fight.

"Do not fear him, he is only here to protect."

"I don't," he whispered, eyeing the large three-headed hound. The soul may not fear Cerberus, but the two were definitely wary of each other.

Cerberus let out a huff, but he also gave Persephone a look she took to mean there had better be a good reason why she was bringing the soul to him and not Thanatos.

If Cerberus had it his way, she was sure he would keep her safely contained behind the gates for all time. He'd taken to her the moment she had bonded with the Underworld, becoming one with it, and he had become as fiercely protective of her as he had the gates.

Following Cerberus through the gates, the mortal warrior drew the attention of the souls nearby. Stopping in their work for the day, they watched her and the new soul as they made their way to the pavilion where the judges would determine his fate.

That was something that had bothered her in the beginning. These three judges, who were barely coherent most days, made the final decision on where souls went within her realm.

In the beginning, she'd questioned them, testing the scope of their power by walking a soul close to an area they were not meant to be according to the judges. It never failed, the soul would disappear from her side and appear where the judges had chosen.

Naturally, she'd never leave the soul somewhere they were not worthy of being, but she couldn't even walk them past an area if the judges didn't permit it. It had bothered her that she didn't have complete control, but with time, she had found herself thankful for it. She'd rather not be the judge of someone's fate in the afterlife. They had a direct line to Chaos it seemed, and she was glad for that.

The judges had been there long before she had taken her place as guardian of the Underworld according to Hecate and Thanatos, and she doubted they would leave while she was in power.

Checks and balances.

However, if a soul, as rare as it was, decided to make their afterlife their own personal vile playground, they were in her domain, and the judges could do nothing; she could do as she wished.

And oh, how she did.

As the judge's pavilion came into view, she wondered where the warrior soul would be sent. She couldn't see any marks on his soul that would make him undeserving of another chance at life, at being reborn, but that was never up to her.

Normally, a reaper would leave the souls there, at the pavilion, allowing them the courtesy to seek a private judgment themselves. Again, she found herself called to join him, yet another difference she couldn't explain from the normal procedure of delivering souls.

Her own curiosity was strong in wondering if the judges might know the reason why his soul had summoned her and not Thanatos, so she didn't fight against the feeling that she should join him.

Stepping up to the pavilion, the warrior soul followed her until they stood before a large platform that the judges looked down on them from. The area was darker than the rest of the Underworld due to the walls along the sides with only a few lit sconces flickering off the dark marble. The judges were blind, and so they had no need for light, but it was so ominous in the pavilion that she felt sorry for all the terrified souls that came for judgment by themselves.

The pale and wraithlike judges wore black cloaks, their hoods down showing their bald heads and wrinkled faces. Though their eyes were stitched shut, and they were unable to see the soul before them, they had magic beyond what even she could comprehend. They could see the past and different paths a soul could have chosen to go, the opposite of how the Moirai could see the future.

They were somewhat horrifying to look at, and it took her a good decade to get over how much they looked like naked rodents with stitched eyes and dark robes.

She could hear an audible swallow from the warrior soul as the judges all turned as one to look at her and the man. As if to show he was not afraid, the warrior soul stepped forward with his chin up, but the heads of the judges turned to her as if they could actually see her.

"Do you wish to continue through with his judgment, young queen? To continue on the path already set into motion through all that is Chaos?"

Unsure of what that meant, she stepped forward to stand next to the soul and faced the judges with him. He wasn't outwardly acting like he was scared, but still she knew all too well how it felt to be alone in death. She could still remember her own moment of crossing over, the beautiful black wings and skeletal figure that was Thanatos taking her hand.

"I will remain for this soul's judgment and will escort him to where he will stay for the remaining time he is a citizen of the Underworld."

Her heart thudded as the judges continued to assess her without actually seeing her in the most unnerving way, but she held her ground. Persephone jolted a bit when the warrior's hand took hers and squeezed.

"Thank you," he whispered, and she looked to him, his eyes glittering in the light of the sconces.

Tilting her head, she saw the shine of a tear on his cheek, and without thought, she moved her other hand to wipe it away. He gave her a sad smile and huffed out a mirthless laugh.

"Long day," he whispered, and she squeezed his hand as she turned back to the judges, happy in her judgment. That she would not allow him to go through it alone.

The judges spoke of his entire life as if they were reading it from a scroll.

He had been born on the same land he'd taken his last breath on. The home he had died in he had built when he married the neighboring farmer's daughter, taking up a life of a farmer, working in the village he had grown up in, instead of continuing the life of a soldier. He had been determined to give his daughter the childhood he had.

It was the very land that all his hopes for the future were pinned on that the men who killed him came for. They had attacked him while he worked the field, and in his adrenaline-induced fear, he had made it to his home where two men were on their way into where his wife and child were.

He'd fought them off, giving his wife and daughter time to escape. After he'd killed the men at his doorstep, the men who'd been left behind by the rest of their own raiding party, he realized the hit he'd taken from the arrow while in the field was much worse than he'd thought.

It had been a fatal injury.

"Asphodel Fields," the judges said as one after the final moment of his life was laid out before them. "You will return to the mortal realm once you've lived a lifetime in the Underworld. That is our final judgment."

Each of the judges disappeared as if they'd never been there, the flickering light of the sconces ominous after such dramatics that were the judges' abrupt judgment and subsequent disappearance.

Leaving the hall, she walked him to the River Lethe where she held a cup of the water out to him.

Taking it in both hands, he looked from the cup to her.

Giving him a reassuring smile, he nodded, taking a drink without saying a word. Showing his trust in her after she had stood before the judges with him.

Persephone watched as his memories left him, his brow furrowing as he looked around in awe and confusion.

"Welcome home. You are safe here."

CHAPTER 4

It was odd how being immortal meant all the years that passed by felt like mere days. It made Persephone question how old her parents would have been when she and her sisters came along. Answers she'd never have since both of them were gone. Her mother to death and her father to Tartarus where he would rot away for eternity . . . hopefully.

It was only her and her sisters now, and oh, how she missed them.

They were each trying to find themselves, find their place walking in the mortal world as goddesses unknown to the people. Each working to explore, hone, and harness their powers without accidentally taking down the mortal world around them.

It was a difficult balance, especially with her sister Hera's temper.

Persephone was fine being in the Underworld, hidden away from the mortal realm, though her detachment from the mortal world meant when she did visit, it had changed dramatically.

The last time her sisters had visited her in the Underworld, they had spoken of a war brewing on a scale they'd never seen before.

Days later, Persephone had seen her largest influx of souls since she'd taken the mantle of queen of the Underworld.

That had been years ago in the mortal world, and as far as she knew, legions were still moving through Europe. Souls came into the Underworld thousands at a time, and Thanatos had trained several of his reapers to be efficient enough to stay on top of it.

Battles were now fought on land and sea, and Persephone was amazed at how Thanatos and the rest of the reapers were able to find all the souls deep beneath the sea.

She wondered in the few moments of respite from her work in the Underworld, something she found happened far too rarely, how the soul that had summoned her, the one she now thought of as *her* warrior, was faring.

On the darkest nights, she could still see the arrow in his chest, knowing he did all he could to protect and save his family. Her mind would wonder how his family had fared in his absence. Had his wife remarried? Did he have grandchildren in the mortal world now to carry on his legacy?

While he was in the Underworld, she'd checked in on her warrior from time to time. From a distance, Persephone would watch as he danced at the festivals in the Asphodel Fields, worked the land, and played with the young ones who came to the Underworld far too soon.

It was one of the few times she smiled anymore since she found it difficult to keep a smile from her face as he lived a life free of worry and guilt.

When she did say hello and asked after his well-being, their words were never anything deeper than the ones a person would have with an acquaintance. Yet she enjoyed his presence more than she had any other in all her mortal and immortal lives.

Persephone wondered at what the summoning, the subsequent need to be near him, all meant. There was not another soul in the Underworld that had caused such mayhem in her mind. None that had the power to stop her in her tracks when she did her rounds, checking on her people.

None that made her heart pump wildly in her chest at just the sight of them.

Yet as things picked up in the Underworld for her, as she found her place as the queen, she had less and less time to check in with him . . . but he was *always* on her mind.

Standing next to Thanatos as he spoke to his troops, their armor glistening in the purple sun of the Underworld, she almost fell to her knees when she felt a sensation that could only be described as her chest being split open.

With only a wave at Thanatos as he jerked and turned to her in concern, she called her shadows, jumping to her study and using her magic to close the doors, locking everyone out.

Stumbling, she clutched at her heart as she fell into a black winged-back chair, tears burning at the back of her eyes.

While she'd never felt this particular sensation before, she knew what it was instinctively. On some deeper level of her psyche where the string the Fates had chosen to connect her to the warrior's soul existed, she knew he was being reborn somewhere out in the mortal world once again.

A depth of sadness she'd never known ignited in her chest and spread throughout her body as she felt her warrior soul's essence leave the Underworld. Where her heart had been felt like a deep cavern of nothingness once again.

Thanatos appeared from the shadows with concern bright in his frost-colored eyes, but he said nothing. He most likely already knew from her reaction what had happened.

For the first time in centuries, she had to bite back tears.

Persephone found herself agitated for months after the warrior's rebirth.

A restlessness stole over her that refused to relinquish its hold.

"Would you calm yourself? I am trying to work on a new potion, and you are distracting me," Hecate murmured as she pinched some herbs she had grown in the little cottage she'd claimed as her own in the Underworld.

Persephone paced through Hecate's eclectic kitchen. The purple and yellow paint, bright décor, and plants growing along every horizontal surface gave her home a comfortable atmosphere.

Hounds of all breeds lay around the floor of the small kitchen making it difficult for Persephone to move about without almost stepping on one of the dogs. The animals' souls always immediately found Hecate when they arrived, and that was that for them; they would never leave her side. Loyal in life to their owners and loyal in death to Hecate.

Normally, Thanatos would visit with Persephone and Hecate as well when the women were together, but there was a war the likes of which she'd never seen moving through the continent of Persephone's mortal birth.

A man had decided he would rule every part of the land between oceans and kill anything that might choose to say otherwise. All because of this one man's conquests, Thanatos was barely in the Underworld for more than a second before he was back out to gather a soul, or several. There were other reapers in the Underworld army that assisted Thanatos, and they were gone just as much.

Thanatos was the one she liked to have there for the souls when they left their bodies. He did more than gather the soul up like a business transaction. He calmed and soothed them.

Due to the war in the mortal world, it was stressful in the Underworld, and as of late, she'd grown more and more agitated. She let her friends and sisters think it was the war and copious number of souls coming in, but she knew deep down it had nothing to do with the Underworld.

It felt almost as if she were fighting off an addiction she couldn't explain.

Slamming down a bottle, Hecate whirled on Persephone.

"Enough! Why are you in such a state? It's been years of you looking out the window to worlds that exist only in your mind. I've been patient, Persephone, but now you need to tell me what is happening."

Persephone couldn't find the words, having been directly asked, and her tongue had suddenly grown too large in size to speak.

"I . . . I am not completely sure." It was the truth. Nothing about the situation made any sense and naturally the judges had nothing coherent to say about it when she did go back to ask after his judgment.

"There was a soul, a while back, that called to me instead of Thanatos . . ."

Hecate tilted her head as she leaned back against the table, her purple dress catching in the light of the kitchen, the purple sun setting for the day and catching on the glass bottles in Hecate's window, the facets of color dancing around the room.

"I think I remember Thanatos saying something about that."

"Yes, well, I was pulled to him and walked him to the judges . . ."

Hecate narrowed her eyes, her glittering rings catching the waning light as she crossed her arms across her chest.

"Go on . . ." She waved for Persephone to continue.

"And when he was reborn and left the Underworld . . . I felt . . . lost somehow, a hollowness inside of myself, and I do not know the why of it."

Both women stared, Hecate at Persephone and Persephone at the floor.

"Could it be like the tales of our youth . . . well, mine anyway?" Hecate started, tapping her index finger to her chin.

"Which was when?" Persephone asked, earning a smirk from Hecate. Hecate would never admit to how old she was. Persephone wouldn't be surprised if the woman was older than Chaos itself.

"Long ago, each person was torn in two, a punishment for the hubris of men thinking themselves gods." Raising an eyebrow, Persephone laughed. Primordials had their own set of rules, and so Persephone was hardly surprised they would have done such a thing to mankind.

"They would be separated by land and lifetimes, but once in a witch's moon, they would unite on the same timeline. Perhaps he is the other half of you, and being the goddess means you get to see him in each lifetime."

"I've never heard that tale." Persephone wondered about it.

"Yes, well, there is a man on Earth spouting versions of it if you ever want to listen. Right now, though, he is busy blaming Zeus for all that nonsense your father left in his wake, and wow, does his story have drama and unbelievably graphic explanations." Hecate raised an eyebrow, her lips quirking. "As we know, Hera is not helping."

Persephone was well aware of Hera and her diversions when left to her own boredom.

Shaking her head, Persephone felt the familiar tug, the sensation so similar to when she was called to the warrior soul once before. Could this truly happen again?

"I can feel him calling me," Persephone whispered aloud in awe as her fingers softly moved over her heart. Hecate pushed away from the table and nodded to Persephone before waving her away.

"Then go! I can actually focus with you gone."

Before Hecate could say more, Persephone called her shadows and found herself on a battlefield full of wandering souls, many of them standing over the bodies they had once inhabited. Cries of the dead wove through the air like a macabre melody, but her eyes caught on a man, older than he was the last time he met his end. This time he had lived long enough for his hair to gray at the temples of his head.

Her heart skittered to a stop when he pulled his knife from his waist and placed the tip of it at his heart.

"Stop!" she yelled, catching both his attention and the attention of the souls roaming the field in desperation to return to their mortal coils.

Running toward the warrior soul, her recognition of him even though he looked completely different was all on account of the string of the Fates between them.

He watched in awe, his eyes growing large at her sudden appearance. His lips moved, whispered words she was unable to hear as she neared, but he stopped altogether when she was close. Calming herself enough to walk the rest of the way, she held her hands up and was thankful when he dropped the knife and bowed to her.

"No, don't do that. Never do that," she whispered, falling at his feet and feeling the burning of tears in her eyes. She was able to blink them away, but her mind spun that this man could bring out such emotions inside of her when she tried so very hard to keep them locked up.

He looked up to her, his own tears falling from the pain of losing the men around him, his brothers not by blood, but by circumstance. Her hands cupped his face and tilted his head until he looked into her eyes, her thumbs wiping away the tears from his bloody and sweat-soaked face as the wind whipped around them in anger at having the essence of death in its presence.

His shaking hands found her hips and grasped them, his hold tight, and without another thought, she pulled him against her, hugging him just as firmly.

A goddess who could barely tolerate another person's touch after losing her life at the hands of her father was choosing to hold someone for the first time since she took over the Underworld.

A sense of healing pulsed through her, and if she were to believe in the Fates the same as the mortals did, she'd think in that touch she'd somehow strengthened their bond. That the string was stronger now than ever before.

A blessing and a curse, she was sure.

"Promise me you will not take your own life," she whispered against his cheek, his hands pulling her tighter against him.

The judges would not take kindly to it, and she could not guarantee he would be allowed another chance at life.

Pulling away, his dark eyes looked into hers as confusion marred his brow. She could understand all too well why. They were strangers, and yet that small comfort was heady and indescribable.

Her small smile dropped when she took in what actually happened.

The warrior soul had not only *seen* her while still alive but could touch her.

Lost to her shock, she hadn't noticed him stand back up, sheathing his knife before giving her a small nod and stepping back. Standing herself, she took in the souls gathering around them, ready for their journey to the Underworld.

Looking away from the souls, she watched as the warrior began to gather himself.

Her curiosity was strong, but she knew it would have to be satiated another time. Right now, souls were waiting to go home.

She opened her arms, allowing his brothers-in-arms to move through her to the Underworld where Charon would await them.

It was something Thanatos told her he did, using himself as a doorway, and thankfully, it worked when she tried it. It wasn't a sure bet, but as the men moved through her, her warrior blinked away his tears, turned to gather his sword and armored plates they wore in the mortal realm during battle, and walked away, his sandals moving through blood and dirt as he walked from the field where he had chosen life over death.

He had called to her without being a soul himself, but his summons was instead for her to take his brothers.

CHAPTER 5

It was mere days, actual mortal days, before she was called to him once more. A wound he had obtained during battle festered, and his body could no longer fight off the infection.

This time he lay on a makeshift cot, a woman and two grown male children at his bedside crying as his body lost the fight to death.

The warrior's soul appeared next to her without her summoning it.

"Are you the angel of death?" he asked, just as he had long ago. Shaking her head, she smiled, reaching out for his hand this time.

"No, I am the one who will watch over you and keep you safe while you find the rest you never had in life."

A feeling of calm stole over her at being in his presence again, a feeling she immediately felt guilty for as his family grieved.

Persephone knew it was dangerous to grow attached to a soul, and yet she couldn't help herself. He was fascinating, nothing like the other souls, and when they were apart, her mortal warrior was a huge presence in her thoughts.

Standing before the judges again, he grimaced as blue light moved over his strong jawline from the sconces in the darkened pavilion.

"Why do they look like a human bred with a rat?"

A cough covered her laugh as the judges tittered much like she would imagine a rat might.

"They can hear you," she whispered, but a small smile made it difficult to continue keeping the serious expression she always wore in their presence.

The judges started, and though his uncharitable description of the judges had worried her about what they might have chosen to do with him, the resulting judgment was the same as it had been in his last life.

"By the Moirai, we concede the limitations of the Underworld until all is forgotten."

And with that cryptic message, they disappeared.

Turning to tell him not to worry about the final words, to try to make light of their bizarre behavior, his eyes were narrowed on her.

"I remember you," he whispered, his voice deeper than it had been as a mortal.

Unsure of what he meant, a spark of hope lit in her that maybe his words meant more. Silly, she knew, but obviously weirder things had been known to happen.

"Yes, I came and claimed your soul." It had been less than a day since she'd done so, and he didn't seem so old that he was losing his faculties.

"No, you've come before. I was shot with an arrow, and you brought me here, but then . . ." He shook his head, not noticing how her body froze at his words.

How had he remembered? Nobody ever remembered.

"I feel like I've lived two separate lives . . . It is all in my head, memories from different times, different families, and you." He looked at her, his eyes brown this time, his skin olive, his hair turning gray from the dark brown it must have been in his youth. Nothing like the youthful father he had been the last time he had stood before her in the very same place.

"You call to me for some reason . . . I do not truly understand, but my reaper is not the one you summon with your death or those you care for."

"And you do not truly know why? Why my soul calls to you in its darkest moment?"

"No, I have nothing to go on. I've never been called like this, and the summons started when I was only just starting my life as the guardian of the Underworld."

Looking out toward the purple sun as it lowered in the sky, he took a deep breath. His eyes searched for something on the horizon only he could see.

Having been watching him so intently, she jumped when his hand found hers. Staring at their hands, she was fascinated as she let him entangle their fingers together.

In her mind, she could see fate doing the same to their own tangled threads of existence.

"Thank you for being the one to guide me, Goddess," he said in a small whisper that had the effect of a loud proclamation with how it made her heart pound.

Perhaps this would be the last time they met, but as his hand held hers as she guided him to the River Lethe, she hoped not.

It was one of the only things she had to look forward to in her now very long and monotonous life.

CHAPTER 6

The days passed by far too quickly when he was within her realm. She tried to keep her mind occupied, holding court and even hosting some balls for her people to enjoy themselves, but he was always there, his presence tugging at her, begging her to come see him.

While it was not the same physical tug she felt in her chest when his soul called upon death, it was just as strong. The emotional connection she felt with the soul even after he lost his memories was almost too much to bear some days.

He wouldn't remember her, would only know her as the queen of the realm, but she couldn't help herself. Persephone checked in on him at least once a day, just to see for herself he was doing well. She wanted to make sure he was thriving and without any issues before he went back out to battle the perils that always awaited him in the mortal world.

Watching him was the only time she felt a lightness in her soul in the long, dark hours that her life was becoming.

She loved watching over her souls, she could admit that much, but she was missing out on companionship. Something more than her guardianship with the Underworld and other relationships could ever be.

"Persephone?" Her attention moved to the man walking toward her from the River Cocytus, his dark eyes questioning where she had gone in her mind. Something she found herself apologizing for more and more, her distraction and thinking of her mortal warrior when in the company of a potential lover.

The new river demigod, Tristan, had shown interest, but she couldn't get her warrior out of her mind long enough to engage with the river demigod in any meaningful way.

"I was—"

"Thinking of someone else again?" Tristan smiled at her, but she knew he was hurt, too, even though she'd never been anything less than honest with him. If they did anything, it would be more of a biological release, a physical relationship.

No, she couldn't move past the connection her soul had with another. Every man would fail in comparison to her mortal warrior.

"Yes, I . . ." She never knew what to say and wondered why Tristan even bothered to continue in his pursuit of her.

"I told you, nothing more than sex has to happen." He smiled again, taking her hand in his, stroking his thumb over the back of her hand.

It was tempting. *So very tempting.*

A bored snort left one of Cerberus's heads from where he lay down near where Persephone stood. They'd been walking, checking over the realm, when she'd been lost to her thoughts and interrupted their little adventure as they looked over the Underworld.

Cerberus was not a fan of Tristan on the best of days, so the extra delay to the hound's snacks and getting back to the gate would not work to further the demigods favor in Cerberus's regard.

The poor hound had to stand there while she watched her mortal warrior in the Asphodel Fields each time they passed through.

Her warrior would look over his shoulder, catch her eye, see her there, and wave. They never spoke since she was far too worried over what she would say to him. No, just having him nearby was enough for her, and she dreaded the day when he would be gone once again.

It was why she couldn't focus today. Only moments before she had been at the gates, watching him walk away, leaving the Underworld for the mortal realm where she couldn't protect him against the atrocities of the world.

As he took the boat back to the mortal realm, there was always a whispered prayer on her lips that they would cross paths again. That he would continue to somehow call her and not Thanatos.

"I apologize—"

"Stop." Tristan released her hand and held his own up. "I cannot stand the constant apologies. I get that I am not your first pick, but if you gave me half a chance, you could find we have more in common than you think. Perhaps we could eventually find ourselves in more than a physical relationship."

And that right there was why she didn't want to give in. The hope he held was dangerous. He would proclaim sex was all he needed in one breath before making a statement such as that in the next.

"Persephone!" Thanatos called to her as he appeared from the shadows, Tristan stepping away from Persephone as Thanatos moved toward her. Tristan had always been a little afraid of her reaper. "We need to speak on something. Underworld business."

Thanatos kept his eyes on Tristan as he said this, making his point clear that this was not a conversation Tristan would be welcome in.

Tristan nodded before turning to Persephone with a small smile and moved toward the water. Persephone watched as he took his other watery form and merged with the river, becoming one.

Turning back to Thanatos, she knew right away there was nothing pressing.

"Saving me, Thanatos?" she asked with a small smirk.

With a sly grin, the reaper bowed before her.

"I am always at your service, my queen. Whether it is an invading army or an annoying and relentless suitor."

As he stood back up, his black hair fell into his face, and he met her eyes with his own icy-blue ones, eyes that held far too much mirth at the situation. And not for the first time she wished she could be attracted to him. He was one of the most handsome beings in existence, but he didn't feel like hers.

He was a friend she held a brotherly love for, but a lover? Never.

She knew he was meant for someone else. Who it was, she didn't know as that was only something Chaos would.

A soul mate was precious. Persephone knew the warrior had to be hers, and depression fell upon her each and every time he slipped through her fingers each of his lifetimes.

It was the only conclusion she could come to, that he was truly her soulmate just as Hecate had said.

The timeline just hadn't worked out, but would it ever?

She knew that was a possibility, but even so, her role as the goddess of the Underworld meant nothing could come of it. In the end, it didn't matter.

She wondered how many lives he was going to live since most souls only had a limited number before they found themselves permanently in the Asphodel Fields or moving on to Elysium.

Fear tore through her each time she asked herself if this could be the last one. While she wanted him here permanently, she knew it would be nothing more than the relationship of a guardian and a soul. That was something she needed to accept, that there would never be more to them than that.

No friendship. No companionship. Their roles were far too uneven and stilted for anything more.

The stolen moments right at death were the only times they were equals. It was before she took him into her care that she could stand before him as just a woman and not a queen.

And where she was an immortal queen, he was mortal. She felt no power in his bones when his soul was near her.

Nothing to say that he was anything more than human.

CHAPTER 7

Persephone was exhausted from trying to rein in the Furies.

"We spoke about this, ladies," Persephone seethed, tossing the bones the Furies had left around the pavilion back toward the winged women who fussed as their art display was destroyed.

Hissing through their sharp teeth, Persephone growled as she called on her goddess, and the Furies backed down.

The Furies were working far too enthusiastically in the torture fields for her taste. They always enjoyed their jobs a bit too much. Thanatos was on the road walking toward her from where he'd just left new souls at the judges' pavilion.

"Keep it in the torture fields!" Persephone yelled as she threw a femur at the women, her frustration at a boiling point with the beings.

It was always some new annoyance with them, always some new devious plan they had arranged to make Persephone wish she'd chosen to be a guardian of the sea or sky.

"Hecate told me . . . How are you faring?" he asked, staring at her as if he could crack open her mind and all her secrets would spill out for him to pilfer through.

Turning to him, she narrowed her eyes.

"With what exactly?"

Thanatos raised a brow, he and Hecate sharing that same sardonic look. She was glad his personality was shining through once again, and he was no longer the same bitter man she'd first met. He still had his many secrets, but he was growing and so was their friendship.

It was all she had to hold on to in these moments, and she was so grateful for it. She hoped one day he might find his true mate, the only one who Chaos would allow a reaper to have because of their duties. Thanatos deserved happiness.

"With the lack of answers."

Persephone felt her shoulders fall. She'd been doing so well not thinking of the warrior soul, and when Hecate came to her, telling her she had nothing to go on with the why of their relationship, she'd decided to try to move on.

It seemed the universe would not let her.

Looking away from Thanatos, she tried not to feel guilty about spending the night in bed with the demigod Tristan the night before, but guilt swam through her hearing about her warrior.

"Perhaps there are answers still to be found . . ." Thanatos leaned in as he spoke, as if he were divulging a secret none were to hear.

Calling back her cold, detached persona, she turned to tell Thanatos there was no need to concern themselves further before he beat her to it.

"The Moirai, my queen."

Ah, yes. The Moirai. The Fates. The bane of her sister Hera's existence.

Persephone had only stood before them once when she had taken over the Underworld, and it was a less than desirable situation for anyone to find themselves in.

The Moirai made absolutely no sense, and it drove her mad with frustration to even be in their presence. The judges were equally annoying, but the Moirai could move between two forms that left anyone in their presence disoriented and unnerved. They were three separate people, or they merged into one, and their faces moved through the aging process in a matter of seconds before starting over.

It had driven many a mortal mad when the Moirai had once walked the earth.

A visit to the Moirai was the only true option because where else would she find out the purpose of a soul's timeline than with the ones who created and cut it over and over again?

As much as she shut out thoughts of him after his last rebirth, she was only fooling herself. She wanted, no, she *needed* to know the truth if she was ever going to truly move on.

"I guess I will be paying them a visit, then."

A laugh left Thanatos at the displeasure that must have shown on her face.

"Take Hera with you. I heard she blew apart their spot in the mountain when she last dealt with them. They might be so afraid of losing their new home that they may actually make some sense this time."

Tilting her head, she wondered at his words.

"How would making their domicile explode help in gathering answers? Would they not be irate and less likely to cooperate?"

Thanatos snorted, placing a large hand on her shoulder.

"I forget sometimes how innocent you are. Never change." Pulling her to walk alongside him, his arm moved over her shoulder as he spoke.

"When you blow things up that people like, they get a little concerned about making you mad a second time."

At Thanatos's words, Persephone wondered if she should be more concerned about her youngest sister's antics.

The Moirai stood before a rocky wall since their last domain had been reduced to rubble due to her youngest sister's temper.

Persephone had made the choice not to bring Hera. It just seemed safer for all involved, and when she did inquire about her sister, it seemed Hera was far too busy making a small village fear it was cursed after they sold their daughters to roaming traders.

"You wish to know about a particular string?" Clotho asked, dancing around her sisters to a string along the wall of millions of other strings. They all looked the same, except the one Clotho picked up. That one was slightly different from the others, the weave giving off an almost greenish hue. Odd. None of the others did that, but she kept that to herself.

Clotho was the one who made the string, so she would be more aware of the weave than anyone.

Asking more than one question at a time would spin them off into who knew what, and Persephone did not have the patience to listen to them drone on and on.

"I am being called to this soul's death each time, and I cannot help but wonder why."

Persephone prayed to Chaos that perhaps she might get some form of an answer from the Moirai and that she was not wasting her time. She would rather be almost anywhere else than at the top of the mountain where the Moirai hid away from the rest of the world.

Rumor had it Hera was planning to make a place for the goddesses upon the mountain called Olympus, and Persephone wondered if that was simply to displace the Moirai once again.

"The why of the universe is nothing for a goddess to know!"

So . . . no answer. Sighing, Persephone's shoulders fell. Maybe she should have brought Hera after all.

"Everything in the universe must balance," Lachesis whispered as she measured a string, her focus solely on the task at hand.

Persephone could understand Hera's behavior all too well now. Her own urge to throw out her magic, to bring the mountain down around them, was building inside of her.

She was the less temperamental sister, so that was saying something about how much of an annoyance these creatures could be. At least it didn't hurt to look at them like when she looked at the judges.

"Yes, I am very aware of that, thank you," Persephone replied, trying to keep the sneer off her face. She worked on building a detached, queenly, maybe even cold persona, but it was taking more time than she thought. Thanatos had told her that when holding court, she was giving too much away on her face.

Ice queen. Be an ice queen and let them know nothing of what you think.

"The strings of the Fates are strong, but they must have an end and a beginning. They go between two very important parts of a mortal timeline, life and death, each soul having to be tethered to a time. A place where the ends . . ." While she spoke, Clotho put away the familiar string and took another, forcing it into a circle. "The ends will meet and never end. Must be patient, for when the ends meet, the world will shake. Demons will rise. But you and your sisters will know the universe had a plan for you all along."

"No answers to be had until life takes the final breath and becomes equal to death," Lachesis spoke out as the last of Clotho's words rang in Persephone's mind.

"The two halves have not met, but they will. The strings will merge to crown the king!" Atropos said as she cut the string that her sister had just measured, giggling like Clotho was, and Lachesis joined in.

It was absolutely unnerving.

"Moments before the world tears apart, the souls of the two strings will meet, and powerful they will be."

At those words, the three Fates became one person, the Moirai, aging in seconds, and disappeared from the rocky cliff overlooking Greece altogether, leaving fluttering strings in their wake.

CHAPTER 8

Persephone stood with her back to the door of her room, her face flushed. It was him. Her mortal warrior was here. He always managed to call her, and she could never ignore it . . . until now.

The pain was getting more and more intense, she'd thrown up and passed out, but she managed to make it through the first waves of it.

Sliding down the door, she placed her hand to her forehead and was surprised when it came away with sweat.

Thankfully, she had left Tristan's bed before the summons had started.

She wanted to continue to ignore him. She'd been doing so well not thinking of him over the years he'd been living in the mortal world. The more she ruminated about the situation, the more she realized she was setting herself up for never-ending torture if she were the one to keep moving his soul, to have these hints of a moment together and to have it all be taken away again.

Seeing him once more, feeling that warmth flooding her veins, knowing that he would return to the mortal world again, live a new life, only to forget her . . .

It tore at her a little more each and every time they danced this dance.

Shadows flooded her room and then Thanatos stood before her. He'd made her promise to call him when it had happened again the night he'd witnessed her lose the battle to her feelings. She had torn through the castle in a fit of rage even Hera would have been shocked by.

The moment she felt the pull, she sent out her own call to Thanatos and shadow jumped from Tristan's bed.

Stalking toward her, Thanatos pulled her into a hug, whispering into her hair that everything was going to be all right.

"It never gets easier," she whispered into his shirt. "It feels like torture to know what the end will be."

Stepping away from her, he placed his hands on her shoulders, stooping down a little to look her in the eyes.

"I can take the soul. You just tell me where the call is coming from, and I will handle it."

Why Thanatos always took it upon himself to try to fix all her ills, she never truly understood. He claimed she had saved him, but all she did was die and come back as a goddess. A goddess who had taken the reins over a domain that was left to wither from Cronus's neglect and imprisonment of the true Tartarus, another victim of Cronus's evil.

Shaking her head, she stepped away from him, gathering the skirt of her dress as she took a deep breath. A breath that hurt as her lungs began to burn from the power of the call being ignored.

"No, I need to see him. I don't truly understand why, but I do. I feel I will regret making the choice to ignore it."

That was a lie. She knew at least in some vague way why she had to see him. She knew Thanatos knew she was lying to him as well when he lifted his brow and narrowed his eyes.

Her mortal warrior called to her because even in the chaotic behavior of the Moirai, she knew her fate was entwined with this man's and always would be. Her own soul called to his just as much, but something in the universe wasn't going to allow for her to have him . . . at least not now.

"My mother claims she was ruined for all others once she set eyes on my father." Thanatos crossed his arms as the words left his lips.

"Do you believe her?" she asked, wishing she could ask Nyx herself, but having no idea where the primordial goddess even was in the world made it difficult. She'd disappeared a few years ago, and no one had heard from her since.

"Honestly? No. I cannot see myself being allowed such a thing as a soul's call . . . soulmate as the humans term it. If by some miracle Chaos decided to allow me that, I cannot believe I'd ever be worthy of a soulmark."

It was clear he was certainly a skeptic. She knew of the ancient primordials having soulmarks, the intricate designs on the skins of the wrists and forearms, binding two deities to one another for all eternity. They were also extremely rare and hadn't been seen since the time of the ancient primordials. Persephone had never even seen one, and she doubted she ever would.

"Regardless, I am whole as I am. All of me is contained in this handsome shell with nothing missing." He winked, and she gave him a smile in return, glad he used levity now for her sake instead of going to that dark place inside himself.

The pulling sensation tugged at her, and she felt her knees starting to weaken. Thanatos grabbed her arms to steady her, but she waved him away with another small smile. Calling her shadows, she opened a portal to where the soul was calling her from.

Shadow jumping, she found herself standing over a man so badly burned that Persephone was unable to distinguish his features, but she did not need to see his face to know he was her mortal warrior.

The world around them shook, and a nearby piece of the land fell into the sea.

They were on an island where a volcano was raging and spewing as it dragged the city to the bottom of the ocean in its fury.

"It's time. Let go of your mortal life," she whispered, afraid to touch him anywhere. The burns were far too extensive. The wails of people, children, rose in volume as the earth shook once more and a nearby temple collapsed, the land beneath it sinking and disappearing into the water below.

All around her, people who tried to run were unable to make their way to safety before they were taken to the deepest depths, a watery death that Thanatos would no doubt be on his way to gather their souls.

Her warrior's soul began to move from his body as she held her hand out to him. She took in his long black hair that had been braided back, the cuff on his arm with the symbol of a bull and snakes, his matching tattooed chest. A cloth covered the lower half of him, only just barely. Without delay, she pulled him to the Underworld as the entire ground beneath his mortal vessel sank to the bottom of the ocean, pulling his body to join the rest of his people in their watery graves.

Persephone didn't bother stopping at the gates, just continued to the judges, fearful of allowing herself any length of time with him. She focused instead on seeing Tristan later. *The safest choice*, she reminded herself.

Yet as he went in to see the judges, she couldn't make herself leave. Instead, she stood curled into herself as she stared at the pavilion, wishing for some easy answer. Some clue to help her move away from the pain and find a way to live where everyone could be happy.

The moment he stepped out of the pavilion doors, the light of familiarity in his eyes became too much for her, and she turned away, trying to compose herself as she waited for him at the bottom of the stairs. She knew the drill, thinking forward to the Asphodel Fields after a stop at the River Lethe.

Trying to make it as transactional and unemotional as she could.

They had been through several life cycles, and her resolve was weakened by the light of recognition in his eyes each and every time.

Even though he looked so different each time, she couldn't face him and not feel something deep inside of her hurt with an intensity she'd never known before him when he forgot her . . . again.

It took days to recover from each death, yet even when Thanatos offered to go to him in her stead, she couldn't let him walk through each death without her, no matter the pain it caused her, and she needed to accept that.

His footsteps picked up in their pace, and he was running. Unsure of why he was moving so quickly, she turned and was pulled into his arms as he swung her around. Slowing their spin, his lips touched hers before they came to a complete halt, shocking her. He'd never made a move that indicated he felt the same for her as she did him.

"Hey, Goddess," he whispered against her lips, before moving back in to deepen the kiss, every part of her body tingling at the sensation he was sending through her, wave after wave.

Her first true kiss since she wouldn't allow Tristan that intimacy. It was something she never expected from this man yet had always secretly hoped for.

Running her hands through his long black hair, she pushed their kiss farther, lost herself to it. Lost to her emotions for the first time in so very long it was foreign to her, but delicious all the same. This man could easily become a true addiction.

He was home to her. Wherever he was, that was where she belonged.

"What was that for?" she whispered against his lips, her eyes closed as she focused on calming her breathing. Opening them when he didn't immediately respond, she took in his dark-brown eyes. There was so much emotion in his soul that turmoil and desire swirled like galaxies within his eyes.

"I promised myself the last time I died that before I drank from the Lethe, I would kiss the beautiful woman who took such great care of me, walking me through the scariest part of life. I knew I only had a few stolen moments to try . . ." His eyes were full of happiness as he spoke, as if the kiss had unlocked some secret only known to him.

"And?" she dared to whisper.

A smile broke across his face as he laughed.

"So much more than I bargained for. If I could court you, I would, Goddess."

A sadness moved through his eyes then, a sadness she was sure was reflected in her own.

"I've had a taste . . ." His lips pressed gently against hers in a more chaste kiss than the one before. "It was just something I promised myself, to take a taste because . . . what did I have to lose? I wouldn't remember as a mortal."

But oh, how she would remember. She would remember for an eternity.

"Something tells me this will go with me into the next life, memories or not." His admission broke something inside of her. If only he could hold on to these memories as she did, but she had yet to find a way to make such a thing reality.

Persephone watched as his hands went to his chest, something obviously tugging at him, pulling him from her, and as she gathered her faculties, she realized that he was to be pulled to the River Lethe. She'd lose him to the Underworld once again, and for the first time in her immortal life, she was angry and resentful of the place she'd merged her power with and called home.

His eyes went soft, and he laid his hand upon her cheek.

"I will see you again. I promise. Maybe one day it can be for more than a few stolen moments."

An empty promise . . . a promise he couldn't hope to make and keep. They both knew this was all hopeless, but it didn't mean she wouldn't continue to wish for it all the same.

"I hope so too . . . my warrior." At her words, he smiled and laid another kiss upon her lips. She felt the tearing of her heart once again, the one that had only just started to mend, at the goodbye.

It was taking something precious from her each time and slowly whittling away at the humanity she'd strived to nurture and keep alive long after her death.

A coldness swept through her as she accepted that he would be lost to her again, until his next death.

No, she lost all reasonable thought once again when she saw him. She would not be the one to answer death's call next time, instead allowing Thanatos to go in her stead.

Persephone was the guardian of the Underworld, and that needed to be her focus. Her desire for this man, as strong as it was, did nothing to contribute to that. She needed to work to make the Underworld safe and fair, and a queen focused on a soul, obsessed, could not do both.

She watched him take his drink from the River Lethe and forget her all over again before she returned to her home.

A sudden burst of energy flooded through the Underworld as she stepped into the castle library, and just as suddenly Amphitrite was before her, covered in blood and ash. Persephone quickly moved to her sister, catching her before she fell to her knees and shadow jumping her to Persephone's bedroom.

Reevkas were quick with plenty of supplies to clean her sister up, but it was the absolute devastation on her sister's face that had her pulling Amphitrite to her as they had done as young mortal girls.

"They're all gone. I lost my temper, and they are . . . just . . . gone." Amphitrite stared straight ahead as a tear fell from her vacant eyes.

"Who?" Persephone demanded, taking the rag from a reevka to wipe the tears from Amphitrite's face, but Amphitrite only shook her head and curled up on the bed, lost to her sobs.

A flash of bright gold light lit the room, and Hera was there, kneeling by the bed, her hand covering Amphitrite's blood-covered one.

"I tried to save them," Amphitrite's voice was weak, and Persephone and Hera looked to each other before looking back down at the sister who never failed to stand back up after all of life's harsh lessons.

"I was trying to stop humans from killing each other! I was trying!" Amphitrite grabbed two fists full of her red curls as her voice broke with sobs. "I wasn't in time. They . . . I got so mad, and then an earthquake . . ."

Amphitrite let out a howl of rage and pain.

"Give me the rag," Hera ordered, taking it from Persephone's hand before she could respond. Hera always had to be doing something, taking charge in some way.

Amphitrite growled, shoving Hera's hands away before she could help her.

"All of them! An entire civilization is gone because I couldn't keep my temper in check!"

"Amphitrite, you did not—"

"Yes, Hera, I did. I killed an entire island of humans. All of them are gone; not because of human greed, but because I don't deserve my power!" Amphitrite fell back, her hands over her face as she sobbed, curling up into herself.

"Stop that, now!" Hera yelled, shocking Persephone and Amphitrite. Amphitrite only moved her hands from her face, her eyes wide as she hiccupped since her body was unable to just stop her loss of emotional control. "The humans have always torn each other apart, and I swear on Chaos, they get worse every century. You may have lost your temper, but no one deserves this power more than us. We are better than those who came before us, but we will still make mistakes. This one was yours, Amphitrite. Now it is done, and we are here to help mend what we can, but we cannot do so until you stop with this emotional nonsense."

Persephone looked from Hera to Amphitrite and felt some of her own humanity slip back into place. Hera was being cruel, but that was what Amphitrite had responded to best in the past. It did not make the pill any easier to swallow.

"We are here," Persephone whispered, and Amphitrite's aqua eyes looked to her as Amphitrite's lips trembled, but she nodded at Persephone's words.

Hera moved back to sit on Amphitrite's other side, wiping away the soot from her sister's face now that Amphitrite had calmed down some.

Ignoring the sharp edges of Hera while they were in such a state, Persephone reminded herself that the trauma of their past had led them all to their lives as they were, to their powers. That same trauma ignited memories within each sister again each time such devastation happened, and it may never stop being a trigger.

And just like those first nights so long ago, they crawled into bed with Amphitrite between them. Hera continued to wipe at the blood on her sister's face as Amphitrite silently sobbed. Persephone gave soothing words as she pushed Amphitrite's wild red hair from her tear-soaked face.

Each sister held Amphitrite tight as she cast her pain out into the world for them to help carry.

CHAPTER 9

"We cannot stand by while the humans continue on this path," Hera growled from her throne upon Olympus. "Enough is enough."

The very Olympus that had once held the Moirai now held a large throne room with three thrones made of marble.

The thrones had symbols of their powers etched into their headrests: Hera had a lightning bolt, Amphitrite a trident, and Persephone a pomegranate with narcissus flowers.

Her sisters' etchings made sense, but Persephone was unsure what hers meant. She knew the flowers grew at the veil where the mortal world met the Underworld, but Hera had told Persephone she was not the one who chose the pomegranate. Olympus had.

Persephone had been skeptical until she heard the voice of those before her, their power, in the mountain and understood Olympus was more than it seemed. Just as the Underworld was more than a realm.

"While I do not disagree that humans are creating more and more dangerous weapons—"

Hera was quick to cut Persephone off.

"You stay in the Underworld and have no idea what kind of catastrophic event they are working their way toward!" Hera yelled, slamming her palms down on the arms of her throne.

"Calm yourself, sister." Amphitrite stood from her throne, her aqua dress flowing like water down her body, rippling like waves on the sea. Her crown of sea glass caught the light of the sconces lit around Olympus. Night had fallen, and Persephone always wondered if the people below could see them high upon the mountain.

"Calm myself?" Hera stood as well, her white chiton with gold flecks dancing as she walked. Her golden laurel crown inlaid with diamonds was hazardous to the eyes in direct sunlight, but here it sparkled, and lights danced along the marble as she moved. "Are you serious?"

"What can we do as of now?" Amphitrite asked, obviously not paying enough attention to notice Hera's eyes going from stormy blue to gold.

Or, Persephone thought, *she is so used to Hera's outbursts that she no longer cares.*

"We can take over! We can step off this Fates-forsaken mountain and reign over them! As is our job as goddesses!" Hera yelled, sparks of electricity flying off her as she stood face-to-face with Amphitrite.

Persephone called her shadowy magic, having it ready to undo the damage that came from the inevitable fight between her two sisters.

"How? How would we do so? We don't age and are obviously not mortal. Plus, what would we even do? Become guards and roam the city electrocuting people?"

Persephone pinched the bridge of her nose as Amphitrite's sarcasm would only make the situation much, much worse.

"No. We take over the government."

Amphitrite and Persephone both looked at Hera, gauging if she was serious or not.

"You cannot be serious," Amphitrite whispered.

"Oh, I am, dear sister. I am. If the goddesses reign, instead of stepping in once there is a problem, we can head off any disaster the humans can think up in their tiny little mortal brains."

Amphitrite's head snapped to the side, looking at Persephone.

"Talk some sense into your sister before I drown her," Amphitrite growled before she looked back at Hera. "You would take their free will from them? We are not meant to live among them!"

Hera only laughed.

"Free will? To do what? Murder and massacre each other?"

"They don't only kill each other! They—"

"Hera, we cannot intervene. You know such a choice is a slippery slope to what our father became," Persephone finally said. "Cronus walked among the humans, playing with them, and look where that found him?"

Saying their father's name was enough that Hera and Amphitrite both backed down, their power regressing until they were only her sisters once more. The goddesses inside themselves going silent.

No one wanted a repeat of their father's sins.

Hera nodded, one of the few times she'd backed down from what she wanted, or something she was passionate about.

"Yes, well, we will need to keep a closer eye on them, then . . . from atop our little mountain." The last words were said with vehemence before her light ignited the room as she opened a portal and did a light jump to wherever it was that she went.

A thick silence hung in the air between the remaining sisters.

"They are growing creative in their ways to kill each other. Hera is concerned with good reason."

Persephone looked at her as Amphitrite spoke.

"I am very aware. I see the state of the souls that come in. Before the judges, they look as they did upon death, but what would come of us being goddesses among mortals aside from making ourselves more powerful? Making ourselves the type of gods that our father became in his greed and lust for power?"

Amphitrite shook her head.

"I get that being the oldest you saw more than we did. You were the one to fight Father off, but don't you have any faith in us? In yourself? That we could put aside our own ego, pull the part of us that is still human to the surface, and help should it come to that?"

Persephone swallowed and called her shadows.

"The idealistic side of me died when the human Persephone did. As did the human Amphitrite and Hera. So, no, I do not believe we wouldn't become him with more power at our fingertips."

"We could!" Amphitrite's eyes begged as she stepped forward, her hands clasped in prayer. She wanted to believe they hadn't fallen so far from what they once were.

"No, we could not."

The shadows wrapped around Persephone and took her before Amphitrite could say another word.

CHAPTER 10

Persephone couldn't do it this time. The lie she told Thanatos was that she needed to hold court, that he had to gather the soul in her stead.

Thanatos nodded, not asking anything further of her. They both knew the lie was only for her.

That kiss from a lifetime ago still haunted her, and she had accepted she needed to break away from whatever this need for him was. It wasn't healthy.

And on some deeper level, she felt she'd betrayed him by spending her evenings with Tristan. Though it was nothing more than flesh meeting flesh, unable to form a truly intimate connection with the man as much as she tried to make it more meaningful. To make him matter in her heart as much as her mortal warrior did.

As she sat upon her obsidian throne, she regretted not going as the pain of the unanswered call tore through her, making it far too difficult to focus on the words of those who had come to bring their issues before their queen.

People had lined up to tell of all the woes in the Underworld, and she was to fix them.

Pale, trembling fingers clutched the arms of her black throne. The soldiers lined up along the walls of the throne room gave her small, concerned glances.

Fighting off the sickness that came with her ignoring the call, she focused everything she had on her people. She'd emotionally separated herself enough from the soul that the sickness was not nearly as bad as the last time she'd ignored it.

As a couple came in to announce their betrothal, having found love in the afterlife, it hit Persephone that the choice she made was once again the wrong one.

It had been a mistake not to go, a decision made out of anger and loneliness, but the feel of him entering the Underworld and moving to the judges meant it was long past done. She had to tell herself that in the end, she had made the right choice. That she couldn't, wouldn't, let herself continue to be hurt for such small moments of remembrance. It cost far too much each and every time.

This time when he drank the water, when his memories left and he was a stranger all over again, she wouldn't be a vulnerable mess, unable to handle her duties to the realm.

This was what was best for the Underworld and its people. As a queen, she'd finally made the right decision.

Her sisters had their own opinions.

Hera thought her an idiot for putting herself through it all in the first place. Whatever had skewed Hera's idea of love and longing bothered

Persephone, but her sister would give some sarcastic comment when Persephone asked, and an outright tantrum if pushed.

Amphitrite thought that a minute of true love was worth an eternity without.

However, they didn't know the whole of it since they were so busy with their own escapades that she hardly saw them as much as she once did. It had been a good hundred years since she'd seen Amphitrite, and last she heard, the woman was pirating away in the South Seas of the mortal realm.

Hera was doing who knew what, and honestly, Persephone was unsure as to whether she really wanted to know.

A loud bang brought everyone's attention in the throne room to the large wooden doors.

Several of her soldiers who had been casting glances at her were now moving rapidly toward the door. All of them on a mission to see what could cause such a noise.

Her guards were moving into position within the throne room while the guards out in the hall made sounds as if they were engaged in a scuffle.

A yell and some more shouts had her standing, walking through the room but halting halfway when the doors burst open, and a man stumbled in. A man that had obviously just fought his way through her guards, guards that were posted everywhere from the front entry, down the halls, and in and around the throne room.

An impressive feat. One Persephone could respect as she took in the giant of a man.

Tattered clothing hung from his muscular frame. Brown hair was tied back at his neck, but several strands fell into his face from the fight. His eyes were cold and menacing enough that he could have cut through anyone standing in his way without words or actions.

That was until his eyes caught hers. She watched them soften at the sight of her, and she felt the sickness completely abate.

Awed voices went silent as she took a step closer to him.

She wondered why and how he had thought to seek her out. How had he even known he could?

To put himself in peril for only a few stolen seconds—it was such a ridiculous risk to take.

As he walked toward her, she only focused on him, everyone else fading into the background as he fell to his knees before her. Reaching out for her and grabbing her with large hands that could almost span her entire waist, he pulled her into him.

"I thought you would come for me," he whispered into her stomach.

"I couldn't," she whispered back, feeling her eyes and nose begin to burn, but her hands moved to his hair of their own volition.

"I've hurt you." He raised his head to look up at her before standing and cupping her cheek. He was so massive she had to look all the way up. "If I could stay, could live here with you, I would. All my mortal life, I was so lost. I knew something was missing, and when my memories came back, I realized it was you."

Pressing closer to him, her hand went over his much larger one that held her cheek, and she closed her eyes, listening to the same deep voice he had every time he was given back his memories. It was the sound of *her* warrior's soul.

"That kiss ignited something in me that was simmering under the surface. You were why I could never be content in my mortal life. I had to go into battle each life to feel something, something I only find when you stand before me. The truth, my goddess, is I must have wanted to get back to you sooner with all of my reckless behavior, only I didn't know why until I was given back my memories."

Biting her lip, she closed her eyes as his finger ran over where she worried at the flesh with her teeth.

"We only have these few moments in time, please don't choose to ignore them. To have the strength to live another lifetime, I need to know you will be the one who awaits me." Opening her eyes, she could see the honesty in his own, his face begging her not to turn away.

"I would wait lifetimes for you. I *have* waited lifetimes," she whispered as he put his forehead against hers.

"Just hold on then. This has to be building up to something." He smiled, but she could see how unsure he truly was.

It was so much to ask, but weak as she was, she nodded as his lips gently took hers.

She kissed him back, trying to lose herself in him, knowing the moment would end all too soon, as it always did. Her hand went into his long hair, pulling him closer, ignoring the people of the room who quietly watched in awe as their queen laid her heart out for all to see.

They had all eternity to watch and talk with her when she only had these few precious stolen moments with him.

She felt the tug, calling him away, but they each refused to let the other go. His hands pulling her tighter against him.

He was in the Underworld now, and she was powerful here, perhaps she could forgo the River Lethe, make him her king like she did each night as she lay awake begging Chaos to stop torturing her. She'd met enough trauma in her life; Chaos could let her have this.

Before the thought had passed, he came apart, only air left where he had been.

A soul-wrenching cry tore through her mind, but she bit down hard on her lip to keep the tears at bay.

She had long ago promised herself no more tears.

Persephone wouldn't break that promise now.

CHAPTER 11

I t was torture and torment to wait so many years to see him for only a few measly moments. Persephone had worked to remove emotion from the equation so that the next time she saw him, she could slowly disengage herself from him.

She would hold on to her promise of gathering his soul, but that was it. She could not afford to feel anything for him . . . not any longer. She would treat him as just another soul and continue working on making herself cold and aloof. It was working so far. Tristan had stopped asking for more than sex, and when she did have to go to the world above, people kept their distance.

Persephone hated to see fear on their faces when the primal part of their brain felt death nearby. Now with a mere look, they wouldn't even get close enough to find out.

However, her coldness was seeping into all areas of her life and chilling all her relationships. Hecate had made comments about her growing aloofness, telling her she was concerned that Persephone was losing what little humanity she had left. She wouldn't take Persephone's word for it, that it was just easier to cut everything off.

If she could be emotionally disconnected all the time, she could handle those moments that tried to emotionally rip her apart with much more decorum.

It certainly helped with all the souls coming in due to humanity's continued growth in their deadly skills, creating and destroying in equal measure. Plenty of times she would hear the horrific stories from Thanatos, telling of what they saw when he was bringing souls home and from Hecate when she walked the crossroads with them.

The stories sickened her, but it also made it much easier for her to cut off her emotional ties to her old life and the mortal world.

Due to the lack of care the humans had for one another, she found she had little interest in leaving the Underworld. Everything within the realm of the dead was controlled by her, so the souls could never get away with the greed and lust they fell into when they were left to their own devices in the mortal world.

Only when her sisters called her out of the Underworld did she bother to leave. Mostly it was Hera demanding to see her, to speak with her outside of her "macabre castle of doom."

Both her sisters were daring enough to live among the mortals, to pretend that they were one of them until the persona they wore "died." Then, Hera or Amphitrite would become someone else, completely different from the last. Begin a new life and new identity with all new adventures, Persephone was sure.

The thought of doing that herself made Persephone shudder, but it left her vulnerable to Hera's constant comments about Persephone losing her humanity. She wouldn't admit it, but there was truth to Hera's and Hecate's assessments.

Persephone no longer wanted anything to do with the living.

"There are some bright spots to the humans." Amphitrite would attempt to bring levity to the conversations after Hera threw a fit about Persephone's choices. All Persephone could think about was the warrior soul she cared for among the depraved people that Amphitrite and Hera took down on an almost daily basis as they tried to keep the balance.

While out of the Underworld, the temptation was always there to search for him in the mortal realm, but she managed to ignore it for the most part. Persephone wasn't an idiot. She knew how much it would hurt to see him living a full life, kissing another, when she wouldn't have that with him. No, she was not going to go down that road again.

She'd been spending a good amount of time with Tristan, and while it was not a relationship she was seeking, he did manage to keep her bed warm enough that she couldn't complain. It was almost something real. It should have been enough.

Persephone knew if she ever did fall in love, it would be with an immortal. Humans died far too quickly, and her sisters had to keep whole parts of themselves secret from their temporal partners. That was not a trade-off Persephone was interested in.

It was all too much for someone who was slowly losing their grasp on what it had been to be human. To care for another in such a way . . . it was all becoming lost to her locked away in the Underworld.

The less she looked for a connection to another, the less she felt the urge come upon her to connect.

Only two people, aside from her sisters, still cared to try breaching her self-imposed wall: Thanatos and Hecate. There was still friendship between them, but Persephone had pulled away enough for them to worry.

The nights where she shared some wine with her sisters had become less and less frequent, as they all settled into their new mantles after going through waves of turmoil finding their footing in their respective realms.

Persephone was well and truly alone.

She'd been to a few more of her warrior soul's deaths, keeping her promise as long as she could, until she just couldn't anymore.

They would kiss, he would say how he missed her, and then the Underworld would pull him away, leaving her brokenhearted once again.

Rolling over, she was startled when she felt fingers running across her brow, bringing her fully back to consciousness from the deep sleep she brought on with her draught. One she'd had Hecate brew that knocked her unconscious at the first tug of the soul.

Looking up, she saw him, a small smile crossing his face as she blinked, bringing him into focus.

He kneeled down next to the bed, but she had no words as she looked into his umber eyes. How odd was it that she could be in love with a man who never looked the same.

"No need to get up. I know what happened," he whispered. "I am sorry I cannot stay."

Her heart froze at those words, and she worked hard to raise her emotional shield up. But the words that left her mouth were anything but cold and distant.

"Was it painful?" she whispered, hating that so many of his deaths were long and agonizing.

"It was quick. I was able to get many of my people to safety but unable to save my clan chief." His voice held such profound sadness, she used her other hand to smooth away a lock of his long brown hair. "The people are angry; violence is more than it once was among the humans."

"I am sorry." Her voice rang with sincerity.

"As am I. I wish I had all the time in the world to be with you—"

"I know. It never gets easier. I never forget."

"And I do."

Closing her eyes, she tried to keep the pain at bay. She always prided herself on never showing him how much it hurt each time she lost him.

"Don't let me remember anymore. I will not cause you pain any longer. No more memories when the judges pass their judgment, promise?" His words struck her, and her eyes flew open. It felt like only days since he'd stood before her, begging her to come to his death, to guide him.

"It's the only time—"

"It tortures you. I can feel your pain." He laid a dark hand on her chest, right over her heart. "I will not have that for the woman I love."

Those words. Ones he'd never said before, and yet she heard the truth in his deep voice. But she saw the pain in his eyes of him having to let her go because of the hurt their moments caused her . . . only love . . . real love . . . could sacrifice so much.

As much as it ached to hear those words spoken when their time was so very limited, she felt like he'd freed her. But she couldn't find happiness when it might be the last time they knew each other.

"Promise, my goddess?" His eyes begged as he blinked back tears. Her lips trembled, but she nodded. Persephone knew it was the right thing to do, as it was only hurting her more and more.

Yet fire burned through her at this new promise. The pain and tearing of the muscles of her heart felt like a far more painful death than the one she'd already lived through.

Giving her a small smile, his finger lifted her chin as he laid a delicate kiss to her lips.

"Find someone to love. Fulfill the destiny the tides have chosen for you and do not think of me except in pleasant memories."

His form blew away, being called to the River Lethe as he finished speaking the last of his words. Ones she would hold close to her aching heart forever.

Her hand was reaching out to him as he disappeared before it was consumed by the darkness of her shadows, her only constant companions.

The next time his life ended, she could tell there was a spark of recognition in his gaze as she stood upon a hill, taking in her warrior, the Viking, before her. He wouldn't remember her this time, she thought as she took in his wounded brothers of battle.

She'd made sure the judges wouldn't give him back his memories.

As he crossed an arm over his chest, bowing to her, she knew she would continue coming to his deaths.

That with time it would get easier, and the pain would lessen.

It had to because standing before him on the battlefield hurt just as badly as it always had.

CHAPTER 12

The world was on fire all around her from humans developing weapons that were disastrous, immoral, and downright disgusting in their existence. They'd eradicated so much of the human race that Persephone had put every single reaper in her army on alert. Thanatos was running the show as general of the army and the reapers.

Persephone appeared from the shadows and took in the blackened street. Her hands fisted as she tried to control her rage. The urge to kill what remained of the humans who had created such a weapon was hard to push back. Her inner goddess had never been so angry.

The toxic weapons had sickened the seas and left any remaining land outside of Europe infertile. Europe being the only safe area left for what remained of the population. Even then, the survivors of the human race would have very little with which to rebuild.

The edges of the continent had been destroyed, but with Hera's power, the land around Mount Olympus remained untouched. The disastrous weapons went to the east and west, leaving the other continents annihilat-ed. Nothing more than smoking remains.

That was where she was. The last stronghold in what used to be a large city in North America.

Stepping out onto the crumbling concrete road, she watched the man, her warrior soul, as he struggled to sit up. His body was far too weak and damaged to move more than a few inches at a time. A wound to his abdomen bled out his life's blood onto the road below.

Smoke and dust filled the sky, screams rent the air, but her focus was on the man, lying among the rubble. She knew what had happened, could tell by how he and his friends were positioned. He'd used his body to shield and protect his comrades, and they worked diligently to save him while others worked to push back the enemy, making sure nothing touched him.

It didn't matter. The poison the bombs left behind would kill them all soon enough.

She already could feel his life fading away as his friends begged him to just hold on, and in her anger, she wanted to rage that he couldn't. Their kind did this, and now those like her warrior's soul would pay for it.

Persephone refused to look at the cars, where families going about their business, to practices or picnics, lay dead. Futures taken and lives lost, their souls moving to the Underworld.

She would be helping Thanatos move souls this day right after she han-dled this particular one. This one, who was still so very special to her, even though she had spent millennia telling herself she could remain detached.

Something deep inside her own soul said it was all going to change now, whether by her hand or Chaos.

This war, and everything it brought with it, would mean few, if any, lives were left for the warrior's soul to return to the mortal world and live out. That the next time she saw him, if she did, everything would be different from any time before. Perhaps he'd move on to Chaos, having already lived so many lives, and that broke her heart.

The fact that over time the call to her, the one where she knew his soul was ready to move on, lessened in its intensity. She'd thought she had succeeded in lessening the emotional hold the call had over her, but she was proven wrong each time she looked into his eyes.

Would she even feel the call next time he died? If he was even sent back to what was left of the mortal world.

With how weak it was this time, she had a strong suspicion the answer was no. The next time she looked upon this soul, nothing would be the same at all. She seethed at the possibilities of what it all meant.

Shutting down that train of thought, she watched as his eyes found her across the city made into a battlefield, and he gave her a small smile, his energy waning.

"There you are," he whispered, his friends asking him what he could see, looking around to see if an enemy was moving in on them. She knew it was her he was watching. He always saw her.

She wondered if he remembered her on some deeper level that he was unable to access while in his mortal form, if there was some part of his mind that held on to their time together.

"Here I am," she whispered, her words soft, but she knew he could hear her no matter what was happening around them.

Thanatos flashed in and out nearby, taking souls as quickly as he could. She would need to hurry and help him, even if he were clearing the battlefield faster than she could have ever imagined.

The warrior's mortal body took a staggering breath as he struggled to sit up, but he was losing the battle against death and his body went limp. His breathing slowed, and she ignored the yells of his comrades to hold on.

Finally, his chest went still, and his soul moved out of his mortal shell. Only her eyes could see him as he stepped away from his friends trying to revive him.

Looking down at himself, she wondered what he thought as he saw his sightless eyes staring into the world above him where their mechanical birds flew over them, dropping more and more of the deadly bombs.

Killing so many, and for what? Some man in power getting his feelings hurt and lashing out at the world.

The warrior's soul turned away from his body as he took in all that he was leaving behind. She allowed him time to process that this was no longer his world and watched as he moved back to the men distraught at the loss of their friend and brother. Kneeling down next to them, her warrior whispered that it wasn't their fault. That they did their best.

Each man he touched on the shoulder shook off a chill, not realizing it was him saying goodbye.

Taking a deep breath that he no longer needed, he pushed to stand up and turned to her. As she held out her hand, he stepped forward and eyed it before placing his hand in hers. There was a hesitancy she'd seen growing more and more obvious each time he'd died and had not regained his memories after the judges.

She thought it was all in her mind, but as he finally took her hand, giving it a squeeze, she knew something in him understood who they had been, even if the rest of his mind couldn't.

"I hate what this whole damn world has come to," he whispered as he looked one more time at the life he was leaving, then met her eyes. Persephone could see how much he meant those very words. Even if he was unaware of his past lives, each time he died, she could see the fatigue of a life spent trying to save whom he could while he cried for the ones he couldn't.

"As do I."

Each lifetime, each meeting left them both a little more jaded than the last.

"I guess . . . let's go before I beg to go back." He laughed, but it held no mirth, only sadness.

Not once had he ever begged her to return to the life he had lived. Not in all the times she'd found him, always so tired from a life of fighting and dying for a cause he believed in, even when no one else in his command cared. His sense of justice was something she treasured and felt was wasted upon the mortals.

He never fought for the greed of whatever prize his superiors were after; instead, he fought for the innocents who stood between those same men and what they coveted.

Always trying to protect others and right the wrongs, even when it put him in death's sights.

Bringing him to her.

Turning away, still holding his hand, she pulled on the shadows as the screams of families being torn apart rung in her ears. As the loud explosion that was the last of the bombs dropped decimated the city proper. Taking everyone, including his friends, with it.

It was nothing like the battles he had fought long ago, in fields where no one but the enemy lay ready to fight and die. With each war, the humans moved their battlefield closer to the cities, where innocents were lost in the crossfire, fodder for a war very few wanted.

She was so tired of it, of the state these souls came to her in when they walked past the gates. The young children that hadn't been gifted the full life they deserved because of another's greed and deep pockets.

Persephone was done watching it all unfold. The humans had their chance, and they ruined everything they touched.

Hera was right.

It was time for the goddesses to reign.

Please consider leaving a review for other readers! It is always appreciated!
To get all new content before everyone else, consider joining my newsletter
or following me on social media!

About the Author

C.D. Britt began her writing journey when her husband told her she needed to use her excessive imagination to write stories as opposed to creating a daily narrative for him. Ever since she penned her first words, life has been a lot more peaceful for him.

She currently resides in Texas where she has yet to adapt to the heat. Her husband thrives in it, so unfortunately, they will not be relocating to colder climates anytime soon.

Their two young children would honestly complain either way.

When she is not in her writing cave (hiding from the sun), she enjoys ignoring the world as much as her children will allow with a good book, music, and vast amounts of coffee (until it's time for wine).

C.D. Britt is the author of Shadows and Vines, Sirens and Leviathans, and the upcoming book, Storms and Embers. All books are part of the Reign of Goddesses series.

Stay Connected!

www. authorcdbritt.com

Instagram @authorcdbritt

Facebook.com/authorcdbritt

Join C.D. Britt's Street Team on Facebook for new release information and giveaways